Title
How do you see it?

Author and illustrator
Vera Galindo

Translator
Gerard McLaughlin

Collaborations
Edu Flores, Raquel Garrido

Linguistic advice and revision
Inma Callén

Publication
Apila Ediciones

Printing
Ino Reproducciones (Zaragoza)

Binding
Tipolínea Encuadernación (Zaragoza)

Vera has used digital techniques for the illustrations of this book.

How do you see it? was the winner of the Apila First Print Award 2020

First edition: September 2020
ISBN: 978-84-17028-42-8
Legal Deposit: Z 993-2020
Text and illustrations by Vera Galindo, 2020
©Publication by Apila Editions, 2020

C/ Mosén Félix Lacambra, 36 B
50630 Alagón, Zaragoza, Spain

www.apilaediciones.com
apila@apilaediciones.com

apila
EDICIONES

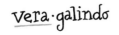

HOW DO YOU SEE IT?

vera·galindo

The other day I discovered
something amazing!

Magnifier

Glasses

Draw

a horse

We don't all see things
the same way.

Estela's glasses

Louis' monocle

Mummy's glasses

Victor's glasses

Mario's glasses

Blanca's glasses

Anna's glasses

Cynthia's glasses

Without glasses

I tried on a lot of
different people's glasses,
but in the end I realised that it didn't matter.
Glasses aren't the important thing.
It's people who see things differently.
Don't you believe it?
Come along with me.

Eye
profile

Eye
straight on

Nose

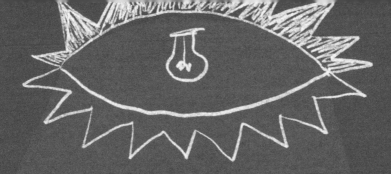

Do you like my striped T-shirt?

Picasso loved them

Does Picasso ring a bell? He used to draw several perspectives in one painting. Crazy!

Van Gogh used to distort the perspective.
He used very bright colours
and brushstrokes with a lot of paint.
What do you think of his room?

Ginger wig

He was missing an ear!
I've got two

Landscape

Portrait

Made bed

Duchamp thought anything could be a
work of ART.
Do you think a wheel on a stool is ART?

ART ~~DOESN'T~~ INTEREST ME

Duchamp stopped
making ART and
devoted himself
to chess

DADA

Is this a
sculpture?

R MUTT
1911

I've drawn myself
a beard
and moustache

Yayoi Kusama sees art
like a kind of therapy.
Her dots help her
improve her health.
They relax her.
Did you know that ART
can help us to relax?

A dot!

Another dot!

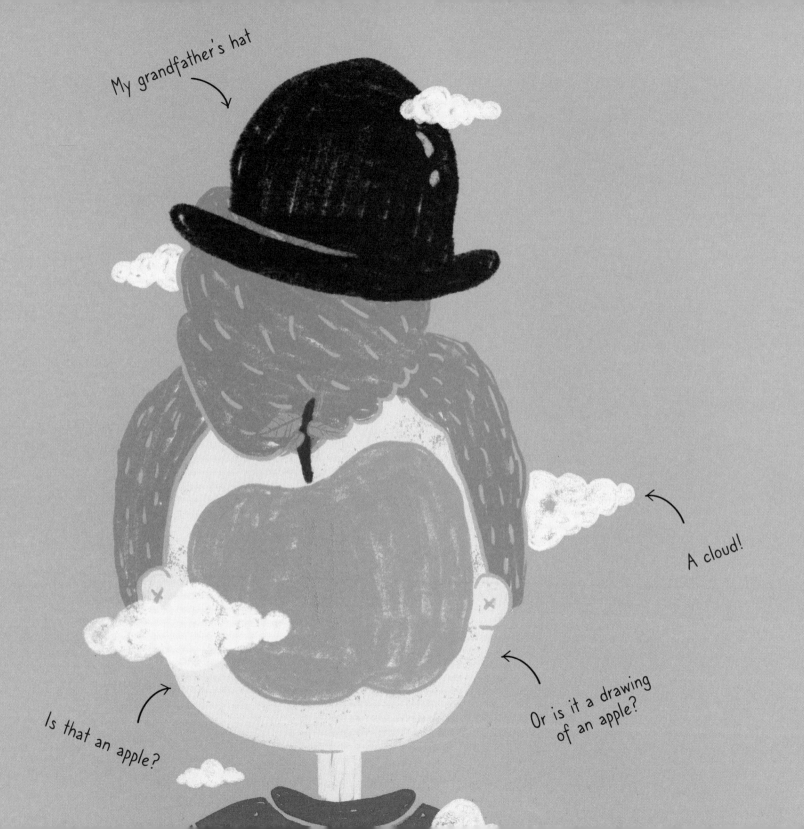

A lot of clouds!

Magritte used to paint
while dressed in
smart suits

Magritte used to paint
his dreams to make us think.

And more!

Frida Kahlo would turn
her sadness into flowers.
I paint flowers too.
What about you?

The comb is my grandmother's

Louise Bourgeois
thought that her mother
was like a huge spider
who protected her
and that's how she portrayed her
in her sculptures.

Banksy is an artist who makes art with stencils and spray paint on the street. No one knows who he is.

What a mystery!

Flowers

Drawing with a stencil

Spray can

Christian

Adrian

Cynthia

ALEJANDRA

And how much fun it is to watch other people draw them!

Christian's horse

Berta's horse

Celia's horse

Adrian's horse

And Cynthia's horse

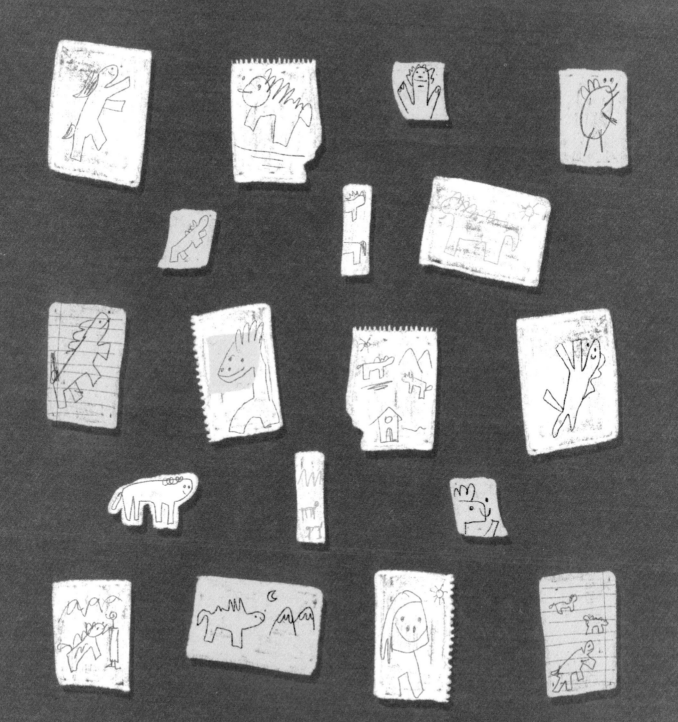